For
Barbara and Mylrea

First published in Great Britain in 2007 by Bloomsbury Publishing Plc,
36 Soho Square, London, W1D 3QY

Text and illustrations copyright © Mike Brownlow 2007
The moral right of the author/illustrator has been asserted

A CIP catalogue record of this book is available from the British Library

ISBN 978 0 7475 7572 6

Printed in China by C & C Offset

10 9 8 7 6 5 4 3 2

All papers used by Bloomsbury Publishing are natural, recyclable products
made from wood grown in well-managed forests. The manufacturing processes
conform to the environmental regulations of the country of origin

MIKE BROWNLOW

BLOOMSBURY
CHILDREN'S
BOOKS

There is a little moon far out in space,
where rockets fly among the twinkling stars.
This is where Mickey Moonbeam lives,
with all his family and friends. Sometimes
though, his friends can be quite a surprise …

It was a special moon-day. Mickey's pen pal Quiggle was coming to visit for the first time. Quiggle lived on a planet far away, and the two friends had never met before.

BIBBLE BIBBLE BEEEEP!

But just as Mickey was finishing his breakfast, he heard a loud noise coming from his inter-stellar vidi-phone – a distress call! Someone was in trouble!

"Help!" cried a voice. "This is Quiggle. My space-scooter has broken and I've crash-landed on to Asteroid B 2672. I'm stranded!"

Mickey pressed a button on the vidi-phone.

"Quiggle," he said, "this is Mickey. Don't worry – Asteroid B 2672 is not far from Moonbeam City. I'll come and rescue you."

Quickly Mickey climbed into his spacesuit,
ran to his spaceship and prepared for take-off.
"Set speed to Super-Zippy-Hyper-Fast," he said,
twiddling some dials. "Thrusters to max!
We have … one … two … three green
lights! Moonbeam AWAY!!"

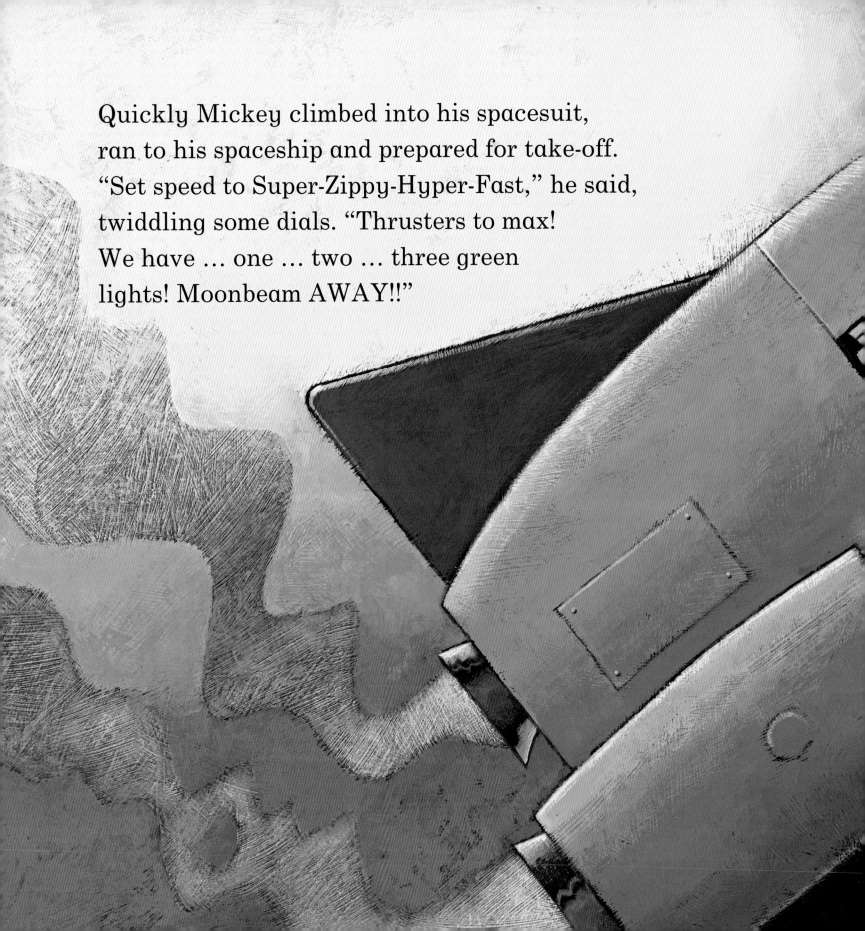

And with a roar, Mickey rocketed up to the stars.

ZOOM!! He flew faster than a meteor, past moons and planets, suns and satellites, and before too long he reached the asteroid.

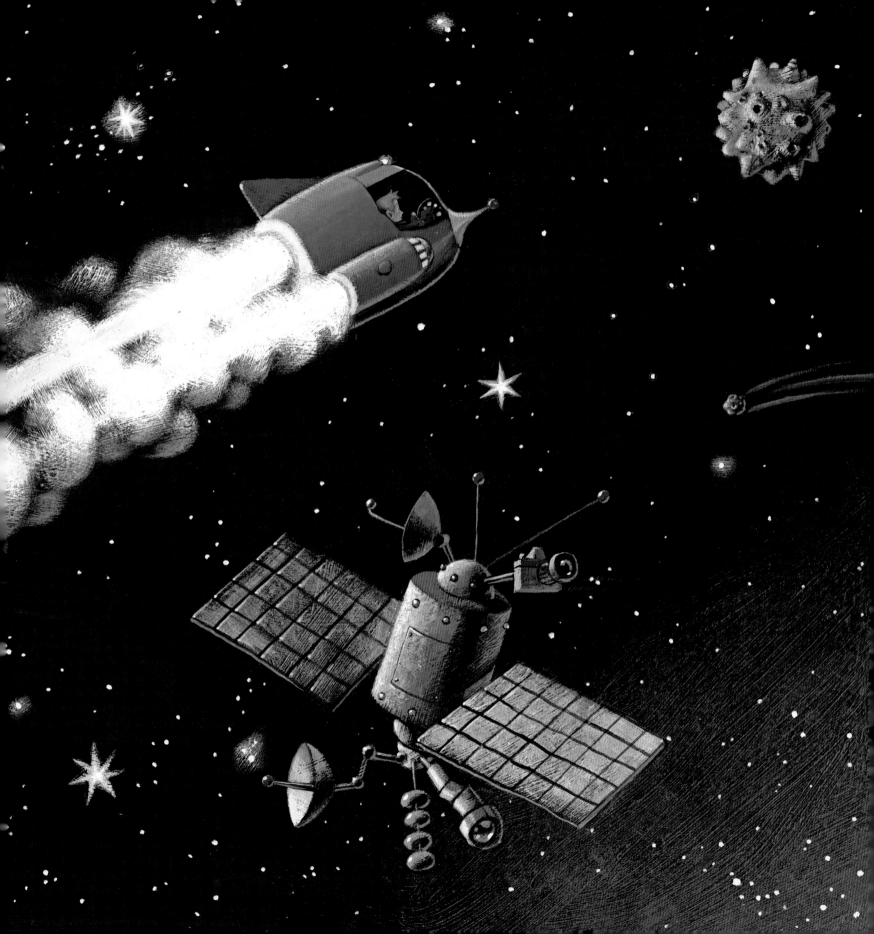

Mickey landed his spaceship on the
large lump of rock and looked around.
But he couldn't see Quiggle anywhere.

He pulled on his helmet and jet boots,
and stepped out of the cockpit.
"Where are you?" he called to Quiggle on his radio.
"I'm here on Asteroid B 2672," replied his friend.
"Where are you?"
Mickey was puzzled.

"I'll fly to the top of this yellow hill to get a better view," he said. But still Quiggle was nowhere in sight. "I can't see you," sighed Mickey. "And I can't see you either," said Quiggle.

Then, just at that moment, the ground beneath Mickey's feet began to move! "Arghh!" he shouted. "It's an asteroid-quake!"

Quiggle was confused.
"I don't feel anything," he radioed back.
"But the yellow hill is shaking!" cried Mickey.
"Yellow hill?" said Quiggle. "What yellow hill?"

Mickey was thrown this way and
that, and began to fall down the
smooth sides of the hill.
Down …
down …
down …
until …

BUMP!

He landed on a small ledge.

Nervously he peered over the edge.
"Great galloping galaxies!" he gulped.
"Are you all right?" called Quiggle anxiously.
"Yes," said Mickey, "but guess what?

I can see a **HUGE** eye

and a **GIANT** nose

and **ENORMOUS** ears

and a **GIGANTIC** upside-down face!"

"And, Quiggle, the gigantic face looks just like YOU!"

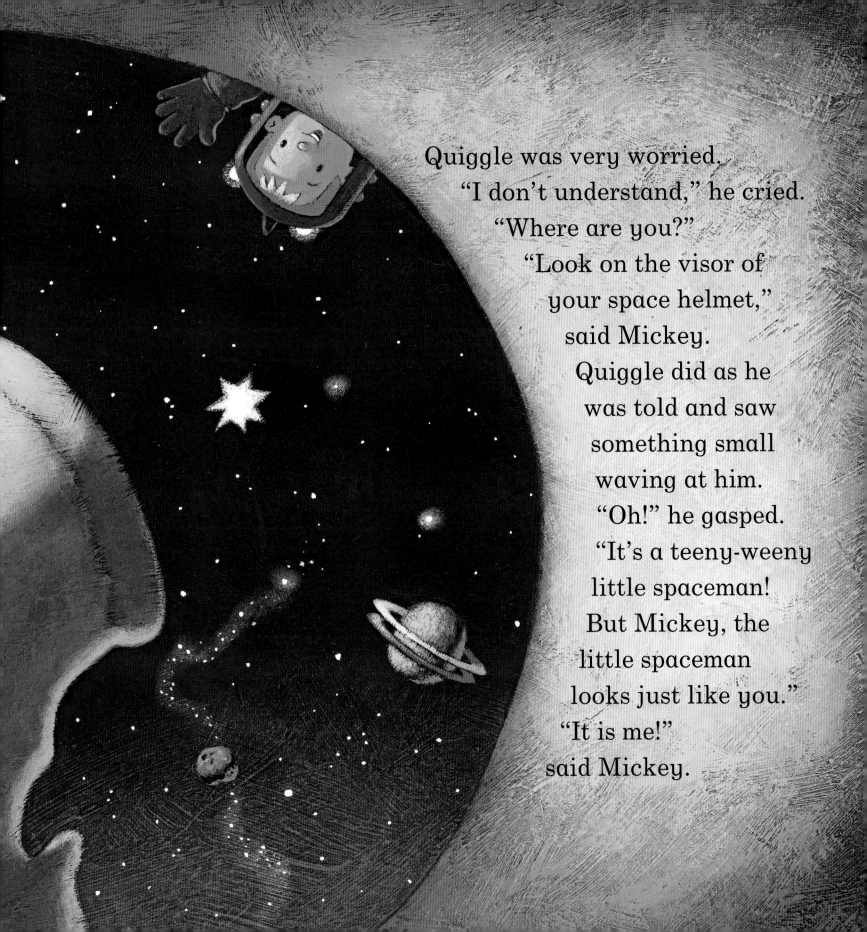

Quiggle was very worried.
"I don't understand," he cried.
"Where are you?"
"Look on the visor of
your space helmet,"
said Mickey.
Quiggle did as he
was told and saw
something small
waving at him.
"Oh!" he gasped.
"It's a teeny-weeny
little spaceman!
But Mickey, the
little spaceman
looks just like you."
"It is me!"
said Mickey.

And then they both understood. The big yellow hill was Quiggle's helmet! "I didn't realise when we spoke on the vidi-phone that you were so small," he said.

"It's not me that's so small. It's
you that's so big!" laughed Mickey.
"If you think I'm big," said Quiggle,
"you should see my mum and dad.
Where I come from, I'm tiny!"

But their smiles soon turned to frowns when they looked at Quiggle's space-scooter. Only one of his engines was working. The other was too broken to fix.

"And I can't even give you a ride home in my spaceship," groaned Mickey, "because you're too big to fit."

Quiggle's bottom lip began to quiver.
"But if we can't fix my engine and I can't fit in your spaceship," he said, sniffing back a tear, "that means I might be trapped on this asteroid for ever. I'll never see my mum and dad again."

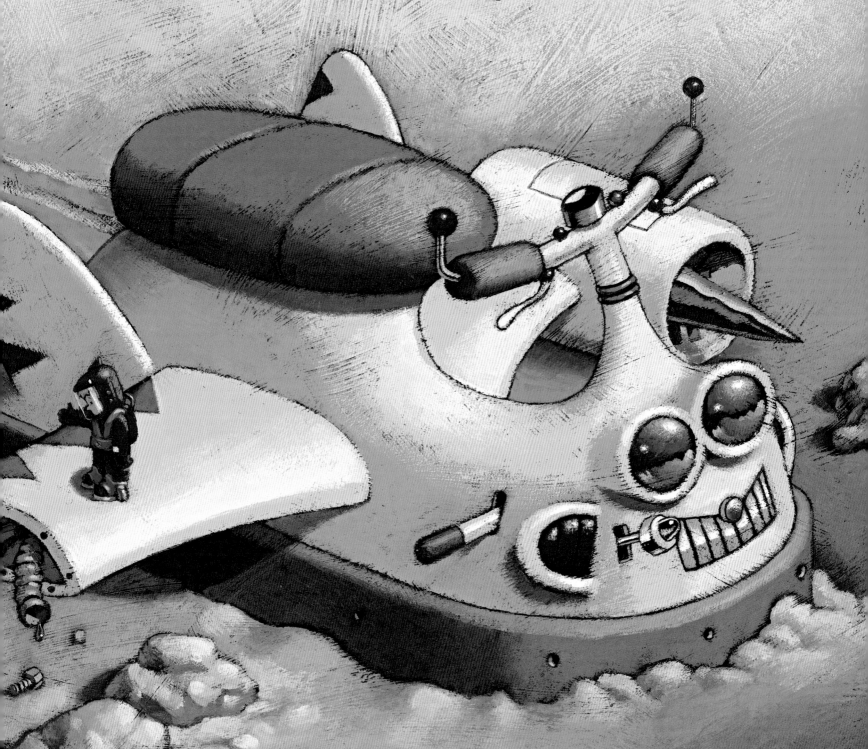

Mickey thought long and hard, then said suddenly,
"I've had an idea!" And he began to crawl
into the cramped, narrow spaces in the middle
of the broken engine.

"Be careful," said Quiggle nervously.
"It looks dangerous in there."
"Not far now," called back Mickey. "I can just
about squeeze through. It's lucky I'm so small!"

A couple of moon-minutes later, he
reappeared carrying a bundle of wires.
"Now, can you move my spaceship over here to your scooter?"
"Of course!" said Quiggle, and he picked up
Mickey's ship as easily as if it were a feather.
"It's lucky I'm so big and strong! What's your plan?"

"Let's use my spaceship instead
of your broken engine,"
answered Mickey. "We can tie it
to your scooter with this wire."
So that's what they did.

"Good work!" they both agreed when they'd finished.
"Now let's prepare for take-off!"
"Thrusters to max!" shouted Quiggle.
"We have … one … two … three green lights!"
cried Mickey. "Quiggle and Moonbeam AWAY!!"
It worked! The two of them blasted off from the asteroid
and rocketed all the way back to Moonbeam City.

While the space-scooter was being properly mended, Mickey showed Quiggle the house where he lived with his family. "The next time you come to visit us," smiled Mickey, "we'll have to make the doors bigger!"